a minedition book
published by Penguin Young Readers Group

Original title: Ein Ball für Alle
English text translation by Kathryn Bishop
Coproduction with Michael Neugebauer Publishing Ltd., Hong Kong.
Rights arranged with "minedition" Rights and Licensing AG, Zurich, Switzerland.

Published simultaneously in Canada.
Manufactured in Hong Kong by Wide World Ltd.
Typesetting in Icone
Color separation by Fotoreproduzioni Grafiche, Italy.

Library of Congress Cataloging-in-Publication Data available upon request.
ISBN 0-698-40049-6
10 9 8 7 6 5 4 3 2 1
First Impression

For more information please visit our website: www.minedition.com

A Ball For All

Brigitte Weninger

Illustrated by Eve Tharlet

Translated by Kathryn Bishop

Max Mouse and his friends were having a wonderful time playing in the meadow.

"Okay, Molly, here comes the ball, right to you!" said Belinda Blackbird trying to help, because her friend, the little mole, couldn't see very well.

Molly's head shot up suddenly, she looked, sniffed and said, "Who else is here?"

Everyone looked around.

"Oh, no! It's Rico," whispered Henry Hedgehog, nervously.
"He's up to something," said Belinda.
"Rico's never nice," said Freddy Frog, sneaking a peek at the dark figure.
"The best thing is to just ignore him," said Belinda.
"Forget about him," said Max. "Just keep playing!"
Max got the ball ready, aimed and with his shorter leg, kicked.

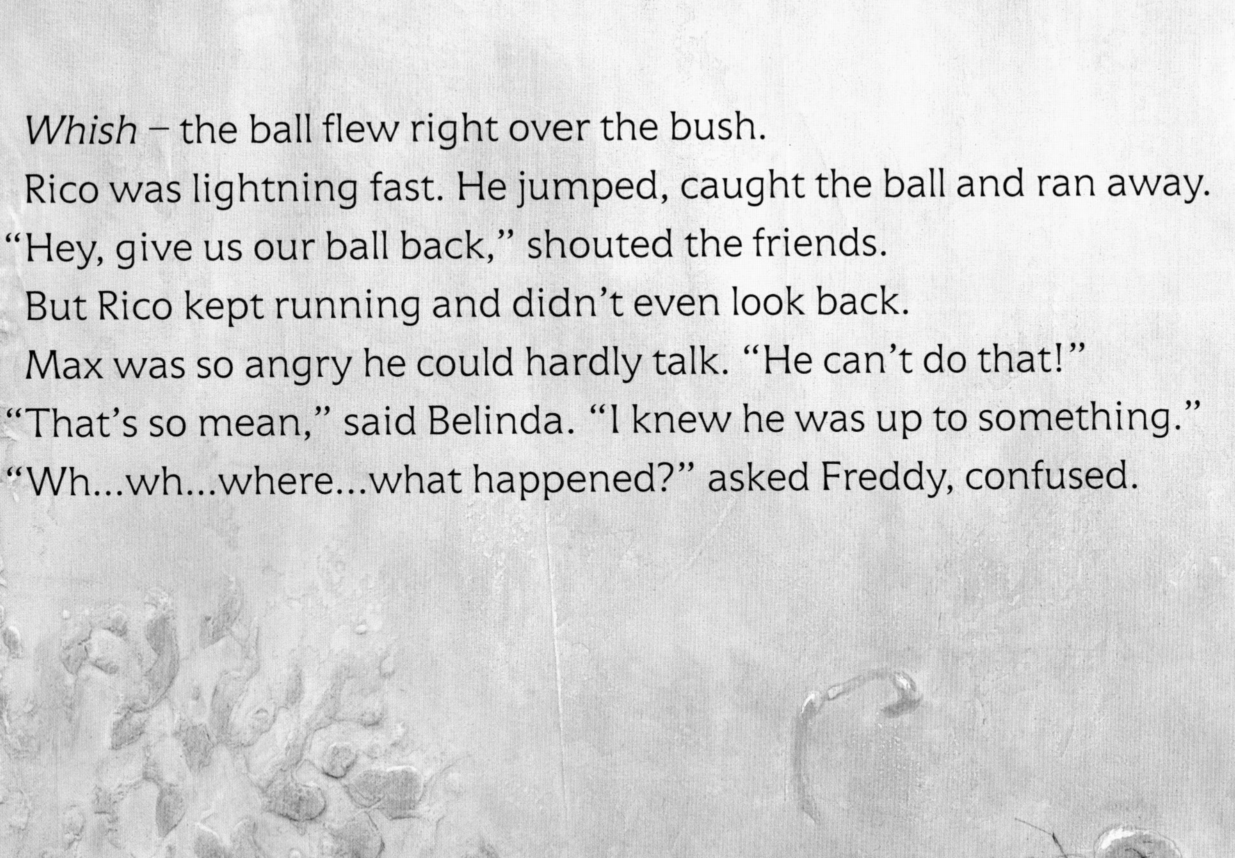

Whish – the ball flew right over the bush.

Rico was lightning fast. He jumped, caught the ball and ran away.

"Hey, give us our ball back," shouted the friends.

But Rico kept running and didn't even look back.

Max was so angry he could hardly talk. "He can't do that!"

"That's so mean," said Belinda. "I knew he was up to something."

"Wh...wh...where...what happened?" asked Freddy, confused.

"I think I can find him," said Molly, and began sniffing.
Belinda was angry. "Just wait till we find him.
Boy, is he going to get it!"

Soon the friends were standing in front of a dark burrow.
"This is where Rico lives," whispered Molly.
"So, what do we do now?" asked Max.
"We tell him we want our ball back!" said Belinda.
"Come on, Freddy."

Belinda pecked loudly on the door
and said, “Come out here
right now and give us our ball back.”
“Ribbit,” said Freddy,
but no one opened the door.
“Maybe, nobody’s home,” said Henry. “I guess
we’ll have to come back tomorrow.”
The friends were upset,
but there was nothing they could do.

Later they sat down to talk about their problem.
"That Rico," said Belinda. "He's always bothering people and ruining their games."
"Why, ribbit, ribbit does he do that?" Freddy asked.
"I have no idea," said Belinda. She was still angry.
"Perhaps we should ask the fox to help," said Henry. "He's the strongest in the whole woods."
"The fox doesn't care one bit about our ball," sighed Molly.
"No, tomorrow we'll go back, all by ourselves."
Only Max said nothing; he was thinking.

The next day they stood in front of Rico's burrow again.
Molly and Henry had volunteered to knock on the door.
Rico's mother answered and asked, "What is it?"
"Uh, uh, could we perhaps, maybe, have our ball back?" stuttered Molly and Henry. "Rico took it away from us yesterday."
Rico's mother was furious and disappeared into the burrow.

"Rico!" she yelled.
The five of them just stood there. What now?

All of a sudden something came
rolling down the long dark hall toward them.
"Our ball!" they shouted.
Max caught it and held on to it tightly.

"Let's go. Let's not stay here another minute,"
they all said.
But Max just stood there, thinking.
Suddenly he knew exactly what to do...

Max tossed the ball so it rolled back down the hall the way it came.

"Hey Rico!" he called. "Why don't you come and play with us? We'll be in the meadow. Bring the ball with you."

The others just stared at him. They couldn't believe it.

"Max, are you crazy?" said Belinda. "He won't come, you know, and we'll never see our ball again either."

"Ne-eh-ver!" said Freddy.

"You never know," said Max as he limped toward the meadow, whistling happily.

But sure enough, Rico did come out, and under his arm he carried the ball, all ready to go.

"Hey, great! Glad you could come," said Max. "It was kind of boring without the ball. Do you want to play? We all have to pay attention because Molly doesn't see very well, Freddy can't hear very well, and I can't run very well.

Will you play with us anyway?"

Rico thought a second. Then he nodded.
"But I'm kind of strong," he warned. "Maybe I should go down to the other end and catch. That way I won't knock anyone down."
"Great idea," said Max. "Let's go!"
The friends played until it was dark.
Rico caught the ball one last time and asked, "Who's ball is this, by the way?"

"It belongs to all of us," said the five friends.

"Does that mean it belongs to me, too?" asked Rico, surprised. "Could I take it home with me tonight?"

"Sure," said Max.

"It's for all of us," they all said. "When you share, one ball is enough!"